This book
belongs to:

....

....

Published in 2015 by Struik Lifestyle
(an imprint of Random House Struik (Pty) Ltd)
Company Reg. No 1966/003153/07
Estuaries No. 4, Century Avenue (Oxbow Crescent),
Century City, Cape Town
PO Box 1144, Cape Town 8000, South Africa

www.randomstruik.co.za

ISBN: 978-1-43230-427-0

Publisher: Linda de Villiers
Editor: Cecilia Barfield
Design manager: Beverley Dodd
Designer: Randall Watson
Illustrator: Jane Heinrichs

Reproduction by Hirt & Carter Cape (Pty) Ltd
Printing and binding: Tien Wah Press (Pte) Ltd, Malaysia

Lynn Bedford Hall is a well-known and experienced food
writer, award-winning author and journalist. This former
teacher has also written a few children's books. Her books
include, *inter alia*, *Hamlet and Pretoria*, *Fig Jam and Foxtrot*,
Best of Cooking in South Africa and *Fabulous Food*.

Jane Heinrichs is an award-winning children's book illustrator
with a BA in Art History and Classics from the University
of Manitoba (Distinction), an MA in Art History from
The Courtauld Institute of Art (Distinction) and an
MA in Illustration from Camberwell College of Art.

Up, Up and AWAY!

For my granddaughters
Alice, Charlotte and Anna
– LYNN BEDFORD HALL

For Mary, my baby daughter, whose
heartbeat inspired each brushstroke
– JANE HEINRICHS

Mattie lives on a farm deep in the heart of the country. It is a quiet place, far from any city. She has no brothers or sisters or friends, and so Mattie was very, very lonely. Until the night of **the secret**. A secret so precious, that only she and her magic, dreamworld animals know about it – and this is how it all began.

One day, Mattie and her mum were walking in the veld, when they saw a big, black beetle crawling under a stone. "Out with you!" her mum scolded. "You beetles eat my roses!" And she poked at it with a stick.

"Mum, no! You'll hurt it! Poor beetle." Bending down, Mattie pushed the stone aside, the beetle scurried away, and **that was the beginning**.

All day the beetle raced across the veld, telling every creature he met that Mattie had saved his life. "Her mother nearly crushed me with her stick! So let us all say thank you by inviting her into our animal world every night when she goes to sleep. We'll share make-believe adventures with her, put lovely dreams into her mind, and when she wakes she'll think of her new friends and never feel lonely again."

And guess what?

This was **the start** of Mattie's magical animal dreamworld adventures ...

"Sweet dreams, Mattie," her mother whispered
as she tucked Mattie up under her duvet.
Mattie closed her eyes and was just nodding off
to sleep when she heard a knock at her window.

"Mattie! Mattie! I'm your new friend,
Ellie the Elephant!
I've just been to Larry the Lion's
birthday party, and he gave me
this bunch of balloons
and I want you to help me fly!"

"But elephants can't fly! They're too big!"
"I know, Mattie, but if you would help by holding the string
while I climb onto a balloon, perhaps the wind could lift me
and I'll go soaring! Up and away!"
"How brave, Ellie! Of course I'll give you a push up."
It was heavy work, but Ellie finally managed
to flop onto a big orange balloon.

"Let's put another one underneath. I'll tie a string to a third,
and if I hold tight, and run fast, maybe a **poof** of wind
will take us both up and away!"

Unfortunately the wind was too strong
for Mattie to keep holding on. She had to let go,
and away Ellie floated, while Mattie landed
back on the soft river bank.

"OOH! AHOO! Look at me Mattie!
I'm flying like a bird!"
But then, just as Ellie was being swept along,
chuckling happily and chatting to the clouds,
there came a sudden disaster!

Two mischievous ha-de-das came flying by.
You know, those birds with long sharp beaks and loud squawks?
"Hey! Look at those balloons!" the naughty birds croaked.
"Waiting to be pricked!"
And with that they popped both balloons,
and poor Ellie went tumbling down to earth.

"Oh goodness!" wailed Mattie in dismay.
"Ellie will hit the ground with a terrible thump.
She may get **very** hurt!"
But luck was on Ellie's side.
Instead of landing in a tree, or on a rock,
Ellie fell on her back into the river.
It wasn't very deep, but even so only her
tummy and her trunk were above the water,
and she was sinking fast.

Frantically, Mattie called for help,
but there wasn't a creature in sight.
But then – **and then** – guess what she **did** see:
a huge hippopotamus dozing; just his head
and his bulging eyes above the water.

Mattie picked up an acorn and threw it,
hitting the hippo on the head.

"Hey Harry! Wake up! Can't you see that Ellie is in trouble?
She needs your help, so please get moving
and give that little elephant a shove from below!"
Harry got such a fright that he rose up with an enormous
splash and, grunting and rumbling,
started through the water as fast as he could.

A hippo's short, strong legs are able to thump along
the bottom of a river at lightning speed, and because
Harry knew that there was a serious problem ahead,
he trundled along as fast as he possibly could.

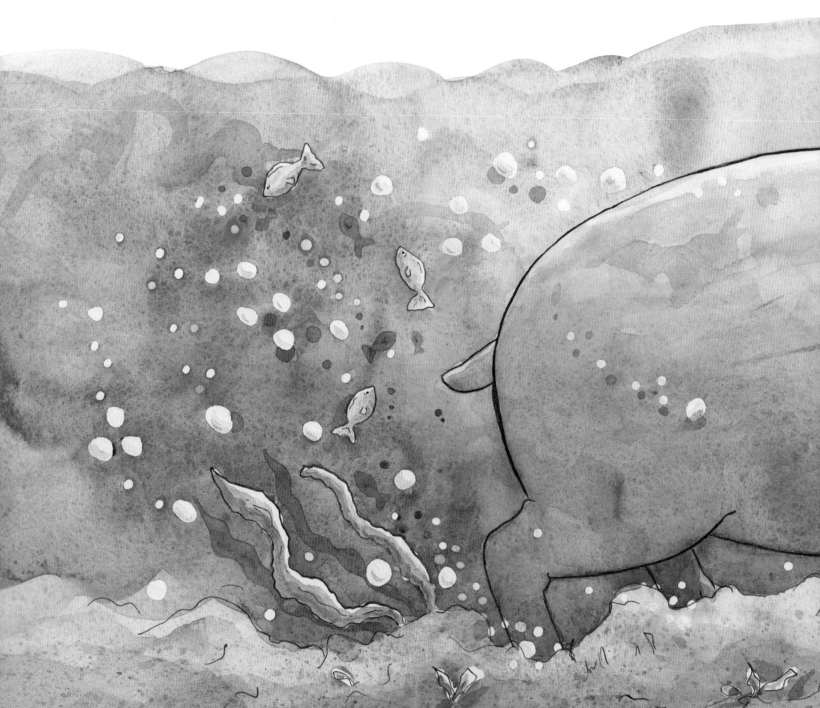

Even so, poor Ellie had almost completely disappeared by the time Harry reached her. Only the very tip of her trunk was waving sadly above the water line.

Now Harry knew exactly what to do.
He would drop his huge head under Ellie's behind,
and shove her through the water to the river bank.
"Phew!" he spluttered. "This is a heavy little elephant.
I'll have to give her a really huge push."
Harry did, and suddenly Ellie's head,
trunk and ears sploshed right out of the water,
just where Mattie was standing, waiting anxiously.

"Thank you, Harry! It's wonderful
to have Ellie safely back!"
Mattie gave Ellie a hug, while Ellie snuggled
her wet trunk around Mattie's neck. "Let me lend
you my slippers, Ellie! You must be so cold!"
"Don't worry, Mattie. I've had the most wonderful
adventure any elephant could have. I've flown.
Almost walked on the moon! And you helped me.
I'll be your bestest friend forever."

"Good morning, Mattie! Did you sleep well?"
her mother asked, arriving with a cup of tea.
"Oh yes, Mum, I had a lovely sleep."
"Did you have a little dream, perhaps?"

"No Mum, not a **little** dream."
Her mother looked disappointed.
"Not a **little** dream, Mum, a **jumbo** dream!"
"Do tell me about it, Mattie, I'd love to hear."

"No Mum. **It's a secret**. A very **big** secret."

For another of Mattie's magical animal dreamworld adventures, read *The Castle of Cupcakes*.